I CAN READ STORIES

GIANTS
AND
PRINCESSES

Judy Hindley
Illustrated by Toni Goffe

Kingfisher Books

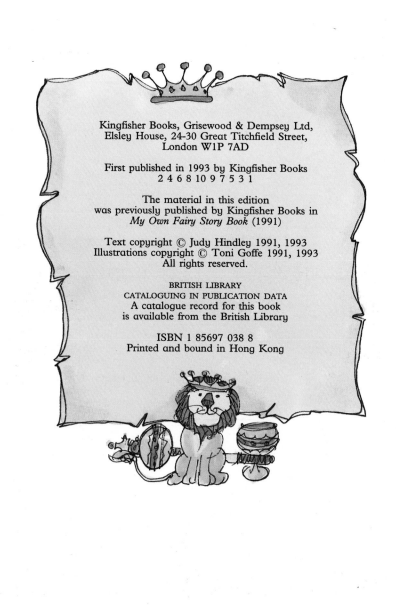

Kingfisher Books, Grisewood & Dempsey Ltd,
Elsley House, 24-30 Great Titchfield Street,
London W1P 7AD

First published in 1993 by Kingfisher Books
2 4 6 8 10 9 7 5 3 1

The material in this edition
was previously published by Kingfisher Books in
My Own Fairy Story Book (1991)

BRITISH LIBRARY
CATALOGUING IN PUBLICATION DATA
A catalogue record for this book
is available from the British Library

ISBN 1 85697 038 8
Printed and bound in Hong Kong

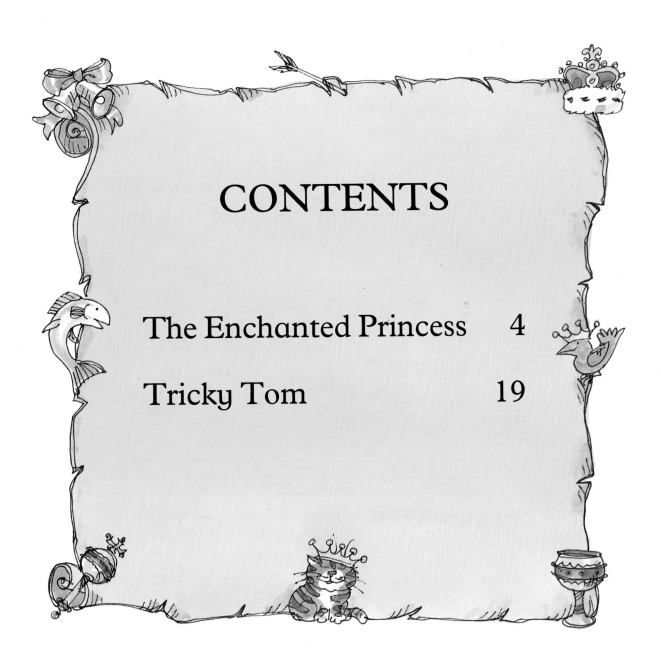

CONTENTS

The Enchanted Princess   4

Tricky Tom   19

The Enchanted Princess

A beautiful princess named Gloriana
was riding in the mountains
with her young sisters.
Suddenly, she saw a wonderful deer
with eyes like stars...

"Catch me
if you can!"
called the deer.

The princess and her sisters followed after.
They galloped and galloped
as fast as they could go.
But however fast they went,
the deer was always just ahead.

At last, the poor horses
could go no further.
"Let's turn back!"
cried Gloriana's sisters.
But Gloriana wouldn't stop.

Finally, the little sisters could go no further.
"*Please* turn back!"
they called to Gloriana.
But even then,
she would not stop.

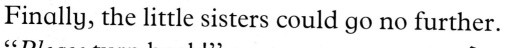

On and on she went
until at last
she couldn't even
hear their cries.

At that moment,
the deer stood still
and waited.
She ran towards it.
"I am a magician,"
said the deer.
"Do you have
any wishes?"

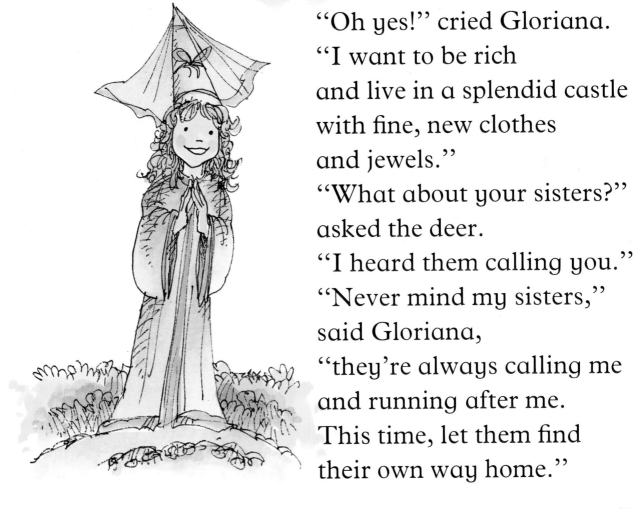

"Oh yes!" cried Gloriana.
"I want to be rich
and live in a splendid castle
with fine, new clothes
and jewels."
"What about your sisters?"
asked the deer.
"I heard them calling you."
"Never mind my sisters,"
said Gloriana,
"they're always calling me
and running after me.
This time, let them find
their own way home."

7

"Very well then,"
said the deer.
"You have your wish.
But someday, *you* will call,
and they won't hear.
Oh, my dear,
you will
cry and cry,
until you are as kind
as you are beautiful."

Suddenly, the deer was gone,
and Gloriana stood on the steps
of a shining castle.

That night,
Gloriana ate from a golden plate
and drank from a golden cup.
She went to sleep
in a golden bed
as big as a boat.

When she woke up,
she found rooms full of jewels
and rich new clothes.
Now she had everything
she wanted –
but there was no one
to see it,
and no one
to share it with.

Time went by.
Soon the splendid castle
seemed very lonely.
One day, Gloriana said,
"I'll ask my sisters
to come and stay with me.
They always do what I want."
Away she went
along the mountain road.

At last, she saw her sisters
in a meadow.
"Sisters, sisters, come with me!"
she cried.
She jumped off her horse
to run to them.

But as soon as her foot
touched the ground,
she turned into
a small, grey rabbit.

"Look! What a dear little rabbit!"
cried her sisters.
As they played with her,
she tried to talk to them,
but they couldn't hear
a single word.

Just before sunset,
they waved goodbye
and went away.

As soon as they had gone,
Gloriana became a princess
once again.
But it was too late,
she had to go back alone
to her grand castle.
"That mountain must be
bewitched!"
said Gloriana.
The next day,
away she went,
by the river road.

This time, she saw her sisters
by the river bank.
"Sisters, sisters, come with me!"
she cried.
Again, she jumped off her horse
to run to them.
But as soon as her foot
touched the river bank
she turned into
a little golden fish.
"Look! What a pretty fish!"
cried her sisters.
They leaned out over the river
to try to see her.
She leaped high
to try to speak to them.
But of course,
they couldn't hear
a single word.

13

This time,
Gloriana cried
and cried,
but her tears
ran into the river,
and no one saw them.

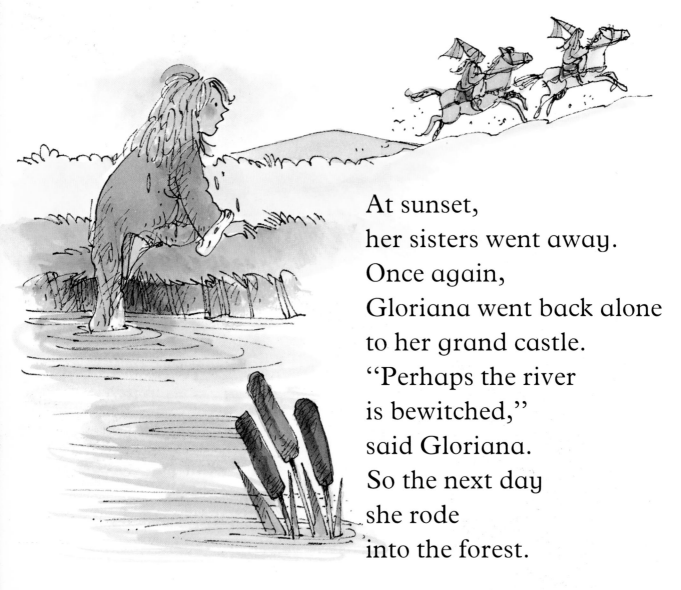

At sunset,
her sisters went away.
Once again,
Gloriana went back alone
to her grand castle.
"Perhaps the river
is bewitched,"
said Gloriana.
So the next day
she rode
into the forest.

The forest was dark
and gloomy.
Gloriana
was frightened.
But
she
went
on.

Suddenly, the wonderful deer
ran across her path.
Her sisters came chasing after it
with a hunter.

They were galloping, galloping
straight towards a cliff.

"Stop! Stop!"
called Gloriana.
She jumped
from her horse
to stand in front of them.
But this time
she turned into
a great white bear.
And when she called,
her voice was a great roar.

They stopped –
and the hunter raised his bow
and shot her.

Down fell the bear,
still roaring.
As it fell,
its roar became
the sweet voice
of the princess.

The hunter raised his bow
to shoot again.
But
the little princesses
heard their sister's voice.
"No!" they cried.
"Don't shoot!
It's Gloriana!"
They ran to hug
the wounded bear
and its eyes filled
with tears.

Then a voice said,
"Don't cry Gloriana."
There stood
the wonderful deer
with eyes like stars.
It said,
"You risked your life
to save your sisters –
you have become as kind
as you are beautiful."

As it spoke,
Gloriana again became
a princess.

Then, suddenly,
the deer was gone
and the sisters stood
on the steps of the shining castle
where they stayed together,
all their long and happy lives.

Tricky Tom

Tom was clever.
He could tumble
and juggle
and do
magic tricks.
And he told
wonderful
fairy tales.

The princess
loved him.
She said,
"Ask my father
if you can
marry me."

So he did.

"Nonsense!"
said the king.
"Stick to your tricks,
Tom!"

But the next day
a giant
came to town.
He stole things.
Everyone ran
from the giant.
No one
was brave enough
to face him.

Then the king
said to Tom,
"Here's your chance.
Get rid of
this giant
and you can marry
the princess."

The princess
was terrified.
She cried
until
her handkerchief
was wet.
But Tom said,
"Don't cry –
I'll do it!"

So she gave him
her favourite bird
for luck,
and she gave him
her handkerchief,
though it was wet
with tears.

Tom went straight up
to the giant.
He said, "I've come
to tell you
to go away!"
Now really,
this giant
was a coward.
Tom startled him.
"Who are YOU?"
asked the giant,
trying to sound fierce.
"Do you know
what I could do to you?"
"Anything you can do,
I can do, too," said Tom.

"Huh!" said the giant.
"Watch this!
I can squeeze a stone
until it drips.
Just think
how I could squeeze
a silly boy!"
The giant
squeezed a stone
until it dripped.

"Pooh! said Tom.
"That's nothing!"
He pretended
to pick up a stone.
But really, he took out
the little wet handkerchief.
He squeezed, and squeezed,
and squeezed,
and of course –

it dripped.

"Huh!" said the giant.
"Well, watch this!
I can throw a stone
beyond that hill.
Just think
how I could throw
a silly boy!"

The giant
picked up a stone
and threw it
over the hill.

"Pooh!" said Tom.
"That's nothing!"
He pretended to pick up
another stone.
But really, he took out
the little bird.

He threw the bird
and it went right over the hill
and kept on going!

Then the giant said,
"Just you wait.
I'm going to pull up
this tree
and beat you with it!"

But once again,
Tom tricked him.

"Quick!"
cried Tom.
"Here comes a dragon!"

"Where!"
cried the cowardly giant.

"Follow me!"
Tom shouted.

They ran and ran and ran.

At last Tom saw a barn
with a very big front door
and a small back window.

"Quick!" cried Tom.
"In here!"
He ran through
the big front door . . .

and jumped out
the small back window.

"Coming! Coming!"
cried the giant.

He ran
through
the big
front door,
and . . .

SMACK!

he ran
straight into
the wall.

Tom skipped around
and locked the front door
and trapped him.

The giant was beaten.
Tom took his boots
and all
his stolen loot,
and sent him away,
limping over the hills.

Then Tom went back
to the castle
and married the princess.
Everyone was glad.

Sometimes,
people asked him,
"How did you do it?"
Tom said,
"Let's go find another giant.
Then I'll show you!"

But they never did –
so nobody knows
but us.

Also available in the **I CAN READ** *series*

Robbers and Witches
Feathery Furry Tales